Seriously Spooky Stories

KINGFISHER
An imprint of Kingfisher Publications Plc
New Penderel House, 283-288 High Holborn
London WC1V 7HZ
www.kingfisherpub.com

First published by Kingfisher 2007
2 4 6 8 10 9 7 5 3 1

A CIP catalogue record for this book is available from the
British Library.

ISBN: 978 0 7534 1498 9

Printed in China
1TR/0407/PROSP/MAR/80NEWSP/C

SUPER SHORTS

Seriously Spooky Stories

Compiled by Chris Powling
Illustrated by Sue Mason

KINGFISHER

Contents

The Bravest Man in the World

Robert Hull

There was once a young man so brave that nothing scared him: not bears, or snakes, or flying arrows or the shouting of thunder.

Not even ghosts scared him.

Outside the village one night, from down by the river, there was a whistling and hooting like owls. "Listen," an old man said, "ghost talk. The ghosts are talking about death and ghastly things, telling ghost stories." His words sent a chill down the spines of the people listening round the fire, but the young man felt only curious to see these ghosts.

He slipped away into the shadows and went towards the river, hoping to find some ghosts sprawled under a tree, chatting in that whistling way that he'd just heard.

He didn't see any ghosts because the three who were there saw him first. They were having their evening meal – the smells of chicken and fish that drifted from the village. Ghosts don't eat; all they need to keep them alive is the aroma of food.

So when they looked along the path and saw a young man creeping towards them they slid off in their canoes, gliding through the water quicker than otters; ghost canoes have holes in them and go faster than the canoes of people. Even the brave young man might have shuddered if he'd seen three misty skeletons speeding along in holey canoes, and if he'd heard the clinky, rustling sounds of paddling bones.

After a while the three ghosts stopped and pulled their canoes up the river bank.

"You know," one of them said, "I think I'll go and scare that young man for spoiling our meal. I'll jump out at him on the path and dance around him rattling my teeth."

"I'd like to do that too," said the second ghost.

"I'll go," said the third ghost. "I'm the biggest, so I'll give him the biggest fright. I'll scare him silly."

"It's not how big you are," said the first ghost, "it's how scary."

"I suggest a wager," said the third.

"Whoever scares that young man the most wins the others' canoes."

"How about a bigger bet? How about our horses?"

"Horses it is!"

So it was arranged. The next night the first ghost paddled up to the village, to give the young man the scare of his life. He walked along the path – pedalling along in the air a foot or two above the ground, the way ghosts do – to the edge of the forest, where the path from the village reached the trees. He sat on a branch and started whistling a well-known tune, swinging his bony legs in time to the rhythm.

11

In no time at all the young man,
just as curious as the night before,
came creeping across from the
village, peering into the trees.

The ghost carried on whistling till
the young man saw him and
stopped. Then – GOOOOR,
GRAAAR, rrRAAAAHHr!
The ghost swung out of the tree
with a howl, rattling his teeth and
whirling his
crackling arms
round as fast as he
could. Then he started
jinking about
and making
hooting noises.

12

The ghost waited for the young man to turn and run. But the young man only listened and looked for a moment, then jumped forward and grabbed an arm-bone with one hand and an ankle-bone with the other. The ghost's hooting turned to a howl as the young man bent the skeleton round into a hoop, and tied it with some grass. Then he started rolling his hoop along the path. The ghost moaned and whined with every clanky revolution of his bones. "Don't, don't!" it yelled.

They came to the river. The skeleton trundled along the path and splashed over the edge.

"You look as if you need a good wash, ghost! Your ghost-woman will appreciate it!" And the young man laughed.

Ghosts can't drown, of course, but this one thrashed about in the moonlit river as if it believed it could. To the young man it was a pretty sight, this ghost taking a bath of glitter. After beating about like a trapped salmon for a minute or two, the ghost finally snapped the grass knot that had been tying it up. It staggered back upright and clinked out, dripping like a fish basket.

When the other ghosts heard what had happened they rattled and shook

with laughter so much that they had
the kind of accident that sometimes
happens to ghosts. They laughed
their heads off: two skulls rolled
down the bank into the river. Two
piles of bones skittered after them
into the water, feeling round on the
sandy bottom until each found a wet

skull and crammed it back on. At first the big skeleton had the little one's skull on, which slipped off; the smaller skeleton went tottering round wearing the tall ghost's skull. It took a minute or two until they had sorted out the right heads.

The following night the second ghost went to the village. When the young man came along the path, the ghost jumped out of hiding and threw an arm round the young man's neck, hissing, "Dance with a ghost! Swing along with a skeleton!"

"I think I'd like that!" the young man said calmly, putting his arms round the ghost. The ghost couldn't believe its ear sockets. It couldn't break free either. The young man's hands had a tight grip on the dry bones of the ghost as they started swaying from side to side. "I'm dancing with a ghost," the young man sang. "My partner's a skeleton. But what shall we do for music and rhythm? I know, your little echoey skull."

And as calmly as if he were taking a pot from a hook the young man lifted the skull off the ghost's neck and put it under his arm. Then, pulling a leg-bone out from under one of the knees, he began to hammer out a catchy rhythm on the skull. "Dance with me, you dumb skull, you ghastly, ghostly, glum skull, let me thump your drum skull, your empty little numb skull! What a haunting rhythm I'm beating on where your brain was!"

The ghost groaned. "Don't, don't, my head hurts!"

"You haven't got a head, boneful ex-person, only a hollow skull. It can't hurt. Ghosts can't feel pain."

"This ghost can. And don't whirl the rest of me round. Don't dance me so hard. I've got dizziness in every bone!"

The young man was whirling the
ghost round so fast that pieces started
to fly off. A finger-bone flipped
through the air. An ankle slid off into
the bushes. Faster and faster. One,
two ribs jangled down into the dust.
The ghost was in pieces! The young
man laughed, watching the ghost
shambling and dithering about trying
to reassemble itself.

The ghost howled. "I shall tell my
ghost-man about your cruelty, and
he will come and scare you out of
your wits!"

So it was a ghost-woman he had
danced with! "Even better! I've
danced with a ghost-woman!" the

young man cried, as the ghost-
woman limped off down
the path, a bone or
two still missing.

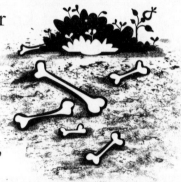

When the
ghost told her
story to the others,
only one ghost
laughed, the third one. He knew how
much he was going to terrify the
young man and win the bet. The next
night he rode off on his large skeleton
horse to find the young man.

The young man was already on the
path, waiting. "I and my horse have
come to kill you," said the ghost in
his deepest, hollowest voice, making

his skeleton horse rear up over the
young man.

"You cannot kill me," the young
man said. "I'm a ghost in disguise, a
witch-ghost with false eyes, false
flesh, false teeth. I'm an illusion. I
can scare you to bits!" And the
young man moaned and howled like
a pack of wolves – HAROO!
HAROOZLE! FAROOZLE! He
crossed his eyes and gnashed his
teeth. He made piercing
whistling sounds.
It would have
sent a herd of
buffalo thundering
off in terror.

The ghost started to moan and shake, limbs going every way at once, like bits of scribble. Then the horse under him began trembling too, and after a few moments of terrible shuddering, with the ribs of the horse banging like a gate, the ghost-rider toppled off with a clatter. Ghosts can't be knocked unconscious, but this one decided to rest for a while, and just sat there on the ground.

The young man was delighted. "A horse! I have a ghost-horse! Goodbye, ghost!" And taking the skeleton horse by the bridle he leapt on its back and rode off down the path.

It was early morning in the village when some women carrying water saw a young man on a ghost-horse ride out of the mist. They screamed and ran, waking everyone in the village. People came peering dozily out of their tepees, wondering what was going on. In the dawn mist they saw a ghost-horse with a young man on it. *A dream left in our heads from the night*, each one thought. They stood rubbing their eyes, waiting for the dream to fade. But it didn't. The ghost-horse with its living rider came walking slowly through the village, the young man looking round him with a great grin on his

face, his skeleton horse creaking
under him from the unusual load.
Everyone gaped as the young man
dismounted in front of his own
tepee.

An old man
came over, the
one who had
first heard the
ghosts talking a
few nights before.

He wanted to touch it, to
see if it really was a ghost-horse. He
patted the horse on the rump-bone.
It rattled. He nodded his head, as if
he understood something. A few
other brave people came across and

stood around. Soon the young man was telling his story, and soon people were believing him.

That night, around a great fire, the young man told all the people how he had put three ghosts to flight and stolen a ghost-horse. When he had told it all once, they asked him to tell the story again.

"He is a very brave young man," people said to one another.

"He must be the bravest young man in the world."

"There has never been anyone so brave."

"No one will ever be able to do a braver thing than he has done."

They nodded their heads solemnly.

There were some children sitting round the fire too. After the first hour of listening they began to get bored. A little girl, who happened to be sitting next to the young man, began playing with a piece of wood at the edge of the fire. She didn't notice when a small wood-spider dropped off the wood and ran towards the young man's foot. It ran up over his moccasin, then went further up.

The young man felt a little tickle round his ankle. He looked down. A spider!

He screamed and put his arms over his head. "Aaaaargh! Get it off me! Get it off me!"

The little girl picked up the spider and put it on her hand, watching it delightedly as it scampered round her palm.

"Look! Isn't he pretty?" she said, holding it out for him to admire.

"Take it away! Take it away!" shrieked the bravest man in the world.

Things That Go Bump in the Day

Tony Ross

Foggy was a little ghost, who lived with his mum and dad at the top of a spooky old house.

Foggy was only born about 500 years ago, so he was a very young ghost. He had lived in lots of places, including a castle, but this place was the best. Ghost families like spooky old places because they make them feel safe. This house had lots of bats

and spiders for pets. There were
woodlice too, but they make rotten
pets. You can't teach them anything,
and they are not very
playful. Foggy
nearly taught a
woodlouse to sit
up and beg, but it
kept falling on its
back and kicking
its legs in the air.

Foggy loved being a ghost. But
sometimes life got a little BORING.
There are not many things a ghost
can do. But one day Foggy found a
book of ghost stories and things
began to improve. The first story was

about a ghost who walked through walls. "That'll be a FAB thing to do!" said Foggy to a creepy slug. And he walked BONK into a wall. All he did though, was bump his nose.

"Shouldn't believe everything you read," giggled the creepy slug.

The next story was about a ghost who walked all over a house shouting OOOOOHHH!, waving his hands in the air and jumping out of dark places. Foggy thought that was a silly way to behave, but he couldn't get the story out of his mind. There was a whole house beyond the dusty rooms where Foggy lived. Maybe wandering around the house going

OOOOOHHH! would be less boring than teaching woodlice to sit up and beg.

That morning, when it was time to go to sleep, Foggy's mum gave him a cobweb sandwich and a glass of slime. Then she tucked him into bed.

"Mum," said Foggy, "what's it like in the rest of the house? Are there any dark places?"

Mum kissed Foggy on the bump at the end of his nose.

"Don't you dare go into the rest of the house," she warned. "The rest of

the house is a TERRIBLE place.
Your dad went there once, and said it
was really scary. He said it was
horribly CLEAN, and smelt of
SOAP, with sunlight all over the
place and lots of knobs on
everything. UGH!" she shuddered.

Foggy curled up, and pretended to
go to sleep. The rest of the house
sounded exciting, just like an
adventure in the book he'd found.

When he was sure his mum and
dad were asleep, Foggy got up. He
went to the door and, making himself
very small, he slithered through the
keyhole into the rest of the house.

Foggy floated at the top of some

stairs. It was true what mum had said. The house was horribly light, with a funny smell. "That must be soap," shivered Foggy.

Slowly, he went down the stairs. He hovered in the air a little, because there was tickly, furry stuff spread all over the floor. He looked around for a friendly bat, even a woodlouse, but there weren't any. "Even the creepies daren't come into this awful place," he said to himself.

With bated breath, the little ghost floated along the landing. His heart pounded inside him, and he was FAR too frightened to go OOOOOHHH! Foggy wasn't a particularly brave

ghost, and by now he was getting really scared. The rest of the house wasn't a good place.

Foggy turned to go back the way he'd come. Then he saw it! If he'd had a skin, he'd have jumped right out of it. It was HORRIBLE.

It was very big, and it was lumbering along clutching a small model of itself. It had blue eyes, with hairs all round them, and matted yellow hair hung in twists down its back. Worst of all, when it opened its mouth to snarl, it showed fearsome white fangs. And it smelt of SOAP.

Foggy reeled. Back along the landing

he fled, waving his arms in the air, and shouting OOOOOHHHH! Up the stairs, through the keyhole, to where his mum and dad sat up in bed, wakened by all the commotion.

"Mum," shouted Foggy. "I'VE SEEN A LITTLE GIRL!"

"Don't be silly," said Mum, cuddling her son. "There's no such thing as little girls."

A Face in the Dark

Ruskin Bond

Mr Oliver, an Anglo-Indian teacher, was returning to his school late one night, on the outskirts of the hill-station of Simla, northern India. From before Kipling's time, the school had been run on English public-school lines; and the boys – most of them from wealthy Indian families – wore blazers, caps and ties. *Life* magazine, in a feature on India, had once called it the 'Eton of the East'. Mr Oliver had been teaching in the school for several years.

The Simla Bazaar, with its cinemas and restaurants, was about three miles from school; and Mr Oliver, a bachelor, usually strolled into the town in the evening, returning after dark, when he would take a short cut through the pine forest.

When there was a strong wind, the pine trees made sad, eerie sounds that kept most people to the main road. But Mr Oliver was not a nervous or imaginative man. He carried a torch and its pale gleam – the batteries were running down – moved fitfully over the narrow forest path. When its flickering light fell on the figure of a boy, who was sitting alone on a rock, Mr Oliver stopped. Boys were not supposed to be out of school after 7 pm; and it was now well past 9 pm.

"What are you doing out here, boy?" asked Mr Oliver sharply, moving closer so that he could recognize the rule-breaker. But, even as he approached the boy, Mr Oliver sensed that something was wrong. The boy appeared to be crying. His head hung down, he held his face in his hands, and his body shook convulsively. It was a strange, soundless weeping, and it made Mr Oliver feel distinctly uneasy.

"Well, what's the matter?" he asked, his anger giving way to concern. "What are you crying for?"

The boy would not answer or look up. His body continued to be racked with silent sobbing.

"Come on, boy, you shouldn't be out here at this hour. Tell me the trouble. Look up!"

The boy looked up. He took his hands from his face and looked up at his teacher. The light from Mr Oliver's torch fell on the boy's face – if you could call it a face.

It had no eyes, ears, nose or mouth. It was just a round smooth head – with a school cap on top of it! And that's where the story should end. But for Mr Oliver it did not end here.

The torch fell from his trembling hand. He turned and scrambled

down the path, running blindly through the trees and calling for help. He was still running towards the school buildings when he saw a lantern swinging in the middle of the path. Mr Oliver stumbled up to the watchman, gasping for breath. "What is it, Sahib?" asked the watchman. "Has there been an accident? Why are you running?"

"I saw something – something horrible – a boy weeping in the forest – and he had no face!"

"No face, Sahib?"

"No eyes, nose, mouth – nothing!"

"Do you mean it was like this, Sahib?" asked the watchman, and raised the lamp to his own face. The watchman had no eyes, no ears, no features at all – not even an eyebrow! And that's when the wind blew the lamp out and Mr Oliver had a heart attack.

The Oddment

Chris Powling

At first, I wasn't afraid of the
Oddment at all. I loved everything
about it – its ragged shape, its
softness and smell, its colours all
faded in the sun.

Where had it come from? Was it
cut from an old dressing gown of my
mother's? Or from one of Grandpa's
ancient flannel shirts? "Never you
mind," Mum always said when I

asked her. "Just think yourself lucky
you've got it at all."

"I do, Mum," I answered.

And I did, too.

To tell you the truth, I couldn't
imagine life without the Oddment.
It was my Best Friend and my
Favourite Toy and my Big Brother all
rolled into one. "Honestly," Mum
would say, "sometimes I can't tell

where that Oddment ends and you
begin!"

I couldn't tell, either. That's the
way it was and that's the
way it always would be.

"Make up, make up,
never, never break
up . . . "

And we never
would.

Not ever.

Even when I
started school it made
no difference. I simply took
the Oddment along with me. "No
problem," the teacher told my mum.
"Cuddlies are welcome here."

"Not a Cuddly," I frowned.

"Well, a Comforter . . ." said the teacher.

"Not a Comforter."

"A Special Thing, maybe?"

"Not a Special Thing," I insisted, stamping my foot. "It's an Oddment."

"It certainly is," the teacher laughed. "But whatever you call it, I wouldn't dream of telling you to leave it at home."

So, all through primary school, the Oddment and I were closer than ever.

Don't ask me why things began to change when I went up to middle school. At first, I suppose, I simply forgot the Oddment – and rushed back up to my bedroom at the end of the day to cover it with kisses. Then, every so often, I decided it was too much trouble to look after it amidst all the hustle and bustle of the classroom. "It'll get lost," I complained. "I won't know where to find it."

"Fine," said Mum. "It's your choice."

And she winked at Grandpa as if she'd expected something like this now I was older.

Of course, this got me so ashamed that for a while I made more of a fuss of the Oddment than ever.

But only for a while.

Soon I was "forgetting" it regularly. Worse still, when other kids came to

play I was careful
to tuck it under
my pillow out of
sight. Once, just
to show it who
was boss, I left it
in the bathroom
overnight – a
wet, thundery night when
normally I'd have lain in bed sucking
one corner of the Oddment so I
wouldn't feel frightened. I slept
surprisingly well . . . till I woke up at
daybreak and found the Oddment
wrapped round my neck like a scarf
and one corner of it actually in my
mouth waiting to be sucked.

No, Mum or Grandpa hadn't put it there. I could tell that from how nice they were about it – as if they would have brought it to me from the bathroom if they'd only noticed. "You don't have to grow up all at once," said Grandpa with a grin. "Bit by bit is fine with us."

"Probably you fetched it yourself," Mum agreed. "But you were too dozy to remember."

"Or you were sleepwalking," Grandpa added.

Mum told him off about that in case he'd scared me.

But it wasn't Grandpa who scared me. I knew exactly who'd done the walking while I was asleep.

After that, I admit, I tested the
Oddment out. Each evening
I stuffed it under the sofa downstairs,
or pegged it to the washing-line on
the patio, or locked it in the toolshed
at the bottom of the garden. But the
instant I opened my eyes next
morning, it was snuggled up beside
me in bed.

It had other tricks, too. One of
them was hiding in my
lunchbox so it was the
first thing I saw when
I lifted the lid in
the dining
hall.

Another trick was wrapping itself round my PE stuff – or tucking itself so carefully in the back pocket of my jeans I had no idea it was there, flapping behind me like a tail, until the other kids pointed it out. "Don't worry," they always said. "We've got Cuddlies, too!"

"You have?"

"Certainly we have . . ."

And they meant it, I'm sure.

By now, though, I was pretty certain that their Cuddlies were nothing like mine. My Cuddly, my Comforter, my Special Thing was a complete freak. What I'd really got was an Oddment. And I was beginning to wonder if I'd ever be rid of it.

So I decided it must have an accident – an accident-on-purpose, you understand. After all, nothing could actually hurt an Oddment. A bonfire would simply burn it up, I reckoned, or a lavatory just flush it away under the house ...

Probably you can guess what happened. Or didn't happen, rather.

After this, whenever my eyes fluttered open in the morning, I found myself sucking something that was thin and frayed with a scorched, smokey taste to it and a faint smell of . . . well, lavatory.

No, don't laugh.

I didn't laugh, I promise you – especially now the Oddment was so  shrivelled and so gristly-looking it reminded me of a stringy piece of meat, the kind you can't swallow however hard you chew. It

didn't feel like a scarf round my neck
any more either . . . more like a strip
of sacking or an old, old bandage.

By now I was desperate, I don't
mind telling you. What really scared
me was the thought that the
Oddment might work out what was
going on – not carelessness on my
part at all, but a plot to destroy it
altogether. What would it do then?

Knowing Mum and Grandpa
wouldn't believe me, however hard I
tried to convince them, I told my
teacher instead. Not straight out,
naturally, in case she thought I'd
gone doo-lally, too. Instead, I wrote
her a story about an indestructible

Cuddly called a Whatsit – the best story I've ever written. And there, in her comments at the bottom of the page, she gave me the answer to my problem:

"This is brilliant – even from a keen storyteller like you. It's so spooky it gave me a nightmare last night! Why did you leave it unfinished, though? Couldn't the Whatsit have been posted to the other side of the world, for example – so far away it could never have hoped to get back? It isn't really fair to keep your reader guessing . . ."

Thanks, Miss.

I couldn't wait to get home that day.

The Oddment

Take my word for it, the parcel I bundled together was safe. Outside it looked like an ordinary padded envelope but inside was heavy-duty plastic surrounding an old tin pencil box of Grandpa's that I'd lashed up tight with industrial-strength sticky-tape. A rattlesnake couldn't have broken out of that lot, never mind the Oddment. Then came the real craftiness. The address I wrote on the label was to a town deep in the outback of Australia.

And it was nearly correct . . . except for the person's name and house-number and street. These I completely made up.

Finally, a stroke of genius, I gave the parcel to an uncle of mine to post for me in America. "My friend wants a USA postmark for his collection," I explained.

Now there was no chance at all the parcel would be tracked back to me. It would be stored away forever in some isolated post office far away, down under . . .

That was three years ago. In all the time since, Mum and Grandpa have mentioned the Oddment only twice.

The Oddment

The first was one Christmas when
we had a really good laugh about it.
The second was last month, on my
birthday, after Grandpa gave me his
present – a yappy, roly-poly puppy
called Spike. "Here you are, already
11 years old," he declared, "and
you've never had a pet to look after
– not counting that old rag you used
to tote about with you, anyway.
What was its name?"

"The Oddment,"
I said. "Spike will
be much more
fun than that,
Grandpa!"

He certainly is.

For instance, I get a present each day now. Usually it's a dog-biscuit or a mouthful of newspaper or a table-mat pinched from the kitchen. Whatever it is, Spike lays it on my bed as if it were some kind of treasure, then wags his tail frantically to persuade me I should take him for a walk as a reward.

Today, however, after breakfast, he brought in something really weird from the garden. It was twisted and crusty and somehow travel-weary, like a piece of rigging from an old-fashioned sailing ship. But worst of all was its colour, which reminded me of the sort of bruise Mum calls 'angry'.

Of course, I recognized it at once, and my heart nearly stopped mid-beat.

There it is behind me, coiled up on my pillow, as I type all this on my computer. I've been here at the keyboard all day, to be honest. The trouble is, though I think Miss is dead right about how unfair it is to leave the reader guessing, I've got no more idea about the finish of my story than I had the first time I wrote it. And already it's getting close to bedtime.

Tsipporah

Adèle Geras

Here is something I've noticed: as
soon as candles are lit, as soon as
night falls, my grandmother, my
parents and all my uncles and aunts
start telling stories, and the stories
are often frightening, meant to send
small shivers up and down every bit
of you. When the grown-ups talk,
I listen. I never tell them my
frightening story, even though it

is true. They wouldn't believe me.

A few weeks after my eighth birthday, my grandmother took me to visit her friend Naomi. Why, I wanted to know, had I not met this friend before?

"I never take very young children to see her. She might frighten them. The way she looks, I mean," said my grandmother.

I imagined a witch, a giantess, or some monster I couldn't quite describe. I asked, "What's the matter with her?"

"Nothing's the matter with her. She's very old, that's all."

I laughed. "But you're very old and

I'm not scared of you."

My grandmother said, "Compared with Naomi, I'm a rosebud, I promise you. Wait and see."

She was quite right. Naomi was ancient. Her head was like a walnut, or a prune, perhaps, with eyes and a mouth set into it. She wore a headscarf and I was glad of that. I was sure she was bald underneath it. She sat in a chair pulled up to the table, drinking black coffee and smoking horrible-smelling cigarettes. She spoke in a voice like machinery that needed oiling. After I was introduced to her, I was supposed to sit quietly while the ladies chatted. I couldn't think of anything worse, so I asked my grandmother, "May I go out into the courtyard for a while? I'll just look at things. I promise not to leave the house."

My grandmother agreed, and I stepped out of Naomi's dark dining-room into the sunshine. The rooms Naomi lived in could have been called a flat, I suppose, but it wasn't a flat in a modern block. It was in a part of Jerusalem where the houses were built around a central courtyard, and four or five families shared the

building. In this courtyard there were
pots filled with geraniums outside
one door, and some watermelon
seeds drying on a brass tray outside
another. A small, sand-coloured cat
with limp, white paws was sleeping
in a patch of shade. Naomi's rooms
were on the upper storey of the house.
It was about three o'clock in the
afternoon. All the shutters were closed.

Perhaps everyone who lived here was
old and taking an afternoon nap. The
sun pressed down on the butter-
yellow flagstones of the courtyard,
and the walls glittered in the heat.
Suddenly I heard a noise in the
middle of all the silence: a cooing
and a whirring of small wings. I
turned round to look, and there,
almost within reach of my hand, was

a white dove sitting on
the balcony railing.

"How lovely!" I
said to it. "You're
a lovely bird!
Where have you
come from?"

70

The bird cocked its head and looked exactly as though it were about to answer, but then changed its mind and in a blur of white feathers, it flew off the railing and was gone. I leaned over to look for it in the courtyard and thought I saw it, just there, on a step. I ran down the stairs after it, but it was nowhere to be seen.

A girl of about my age was standing beside a pot of geraniums.

Where had she come from? She wore a white dress which fell almost to her ankles. I thought, *She must be very religious.* I knew that very devout Jews wore old-fashioned clothes.

"Have you seen a white dove?"
I asked her. "It was up there a
moment ago."

The girl smiled. She said,
"Sometimes I dream that I'm a dove.
Do you believe in dreams? I do.
My name is Tsipporah, which means
'bird', so of course I feel exactly
like a bird sometimes. What do you
feel like?"

I didn't know what to say. I was
thinking, *This girl is mad*. My name is
Rachel, which means 'ewe lamb',
but I never feel woolly or frisky. My
cousin is called Arieh, which means
'lion', and he's not a bit tawny or
fierce. I said, "I just feel like myself."

"Then you're lucky," said Tsipporah. "Sometimes I think I will turn into a bird at any moment. In fact, look, it's happening . . . feathers . . . white feathers on my arms . . ."

I did look. She held out her arms and cocked her head, and I blinked in the sunlight, which all at once was shining straight into my eyes and dazzling me . . . but in the light I could see . . . I think I saw, though it's hard to remember exactly, a flapping, a vibration of wings, and

the krr-krr of soft dove-sounds
filling every space in my head.
I closed my eyes and opened them
again slowly. Tsipporah had
disappeared. I could see a white bird
over on the other side of the
courtyard, and I ran towards it calling,
"Tsipporah, if it's you, come back . . .
come back and tell me!"

The dove launched itself into the
air, and flew up and up and over the
roof and away, and I followed it with
my eyes until the speck that it had
become had vanished into the wide
pale sky. I felt weak, dizzy with heat.
I climbed slowly back to Naomi's
rooms, thinking, *Tsipporah must have*

*hidden from me. She must be a child
who lives in the building and likes
playing tricks.*

On the way home, my
grandmother started telling me one
of her stories. Sometimes I don't
listen properly when she starts on a
tale of how this person is related to
that one, but she was talking about
Naomi when she was young. This
was so hard to imagine that I was
fascinated.

"Of course," my grandmother said,
"she was never quite the same after
Tsipporah died."

"Who," I asked, suddenly cold in
the sunlight, "is Tsipporah?"

"Naomi's twin sister. She died of diphtheria when they were eight. A terrible tragedy. But Tsipporah was strange."

"How, strange?"

"Naomi told me stories . . . you would hardly believe them if I told you. I know I never did."

"Tell me," I said. "I'll believe them."

"Naomi always said her sister could turn herself into a bird just by wishing it."

"A white dove," I said. "She turned herself into a white dove and flew away."

My grandmother looked at me sharply.

"I've told you this story before, haven't I?"

"Yes," I said, even though, of course, she never had. I didn't tell her I had seen Tsipporah. I didn't want to frighten her, so I said nothing about it.

Now, every time I see a white dove, I wonder if it's her, Tsipporah, or perhaps some other girl who stretched her wings out one day, looking for the sky.

Widdershins

Ann Turnbull

When they were almost there, below the granite outcrop, Mr Ashton said they would stop and look at the view.

Michael didn't want to stop; he was eager to go on, to reach the summit. But the others were tired. Rucksacks came off and hit the ground; jumpers followed.

"Can we have lunch now?"

Mr Ashton looked at his watch and agreed. "Let's sit behind those rocks, out of the wind."

Twenty children set to with enthusiasm, unpacking rucksacks, pulling out packets of sandwiches, chocolate bars, drinks cans and crisps.

"Up there," Mr Ashton pointed to the piled rocks on the summit, "is the Devil's Chair. See, where those rocks make a shape like a throne? They say that if you run round the Chair seven times widdershins, the Devil himself will appear."

Michael stared.

"What's widdershins?" asked Paul.

"Wiggleshins, widdleshins," giggled Kelly and Zoe.

"Widdershins," said Mr Ashton, "means anti-clockwise."

Hands waved in the air, bodies turned. "That way." "No, that."

"Let's go!" Paul, Craig and Robert were off, widdershins round the base of the rocks.

"You won't get far," called Mr Ashton. "It's not as easy as it looks. And be careful climbing around the Chair," he added to the retreating figures of Tracey and Lorna.

"What does the Devil look like, Sir?" asked Jane, a little anxiously.

"Horns and a tail," said Zoe with relish.

"Maybe." Mr Ashton smiled. "But they say he can disguise himself. Sometimes he appears as a raven, a black dog or a toad."

"Ugh!" said Zoe and Kelly in unison.

The class began to disperse; some went to the edge and began drawing the view; others were dutifully filling in their question sheets;

the more adventurous swarmed up
and around the Devil's Chair.

Michael turned widdershins.

Mr Ashton was right. The going
was hard, and it was not obvious
where to go. Michael had to keep
looking up at the Chair to make sure
it was still on his left; but he couldn't
always get close to it, and sometimes
the lie of the land took him far away,
and he found himself clambering
over piled boulders that looked as if
they had tumbled down from the
summit in a storm. And it was hot;
even in the wind it was hot. Only
sometimes, in the lee of a rock, the
wind would drop instantly, and then

there was a chill, a stillness, and silence. Silence, and then, far away it seemed, a thin piping of children's voices, like distant birds.

He struggled on. The hardest part was just below the Chair, where the land fell away steeply in a scree. Michael slithered, and once he slid several yards, grabbing at pebbles that rolled under his hands before he could scramble back to the safety of the big rocks.

But at last he had completed one revolution. He stepped out, dirty and bruised, and came upon sunshine, and voices and clipboarded papers flapping in the wind, and litter-

conscious Zoe
chasing crisp
packets.

Michael pushed
back the damp hair
from his forehead.

One, he thought. Six to go.

"Michael," said Mr Ashton, "don't
forget you're going to draw the view.
And there's your questionnaire to
fill in."

Michael edged away. "I'm going
round again, Sir."

"Well . . . remind the others if you
see them."

Halfway round the second time
Michael caught up with Craig, Paul

and Robert, who were resting.

"Given up?" he asked.

They wouldn't admit that. "Going up to the Chair."

They tried to make it sound like a better idea than carrying on, but Michael wasn't tempted. Seven times widdershins and you'd raise the Devil. He had to complete the experiment; he had to see if it worked. Michael liked experiments. They were the only things he was enthusiastic about at school.

He went round again. And again.
It was hard. His legs and shoulders
ached. His hands were cut and
scraped as he scrambled over the
rocks. The boys had left the Devil's
Chair but some girls were climbing
on it, shouting, the wind slapping
their hair across their faces.

Four times. More than halfway. He
could do it. He had to do it.

Five times. Michael was exhausted.
It was no easy job, raising the Devil.
He wondered if it had been done
before. You'd have to be desperate
and believe in it.

I don't believe in it, Michael thought.
And yet he needed to be sure. He

couldn't let an opportunity like this pass. Test the theory. Go on. Finish.

Six times. Michael lay spread-eagled on the grass, panting. It was hot – so hot. His whole body ached. The sky glared and the rocks shimmered.

Mr Ashton called, "Michael! We're packing up in a minute. If you want to draw your view you'd better be quick."

"Just once – once more, Sir!" Michael jumped up and was away before Mr Ashton could call him back.

But someone ran after him; a hand touched his arm. He turned. Jane.

"Don't go," she said.

Jane was small and quiet. She had

never spoken to Michael before.

"Six," said Michael. "One more.
I've got to."

Jane gripped
his arm. "Please.
Stop now."

Michael
shook her off.
He heard her
calling after him as he struck out on
his seventh lap.

It seemed quicker, easier than the
others. Like the last stretch of a race,
when you know you've won. He
seemed to glide over the piled
boulders and up and down the crags
and gullies and across the scree, and

suddenly he was back. He felt elated. He had done it; he had finished. Seven times widdershins – but where was the Devil?

Michael sprang down and rolled on the grass. The other children cheered. Except Jane. Michael noticed her looking up at the rocks, scared. But Mr Ashton smiled. "Well done, Michael. Pack up your bags now, everyone. It's time to go."

They heaved up their rucksacks and removed the last scraps of litter. As they turned towards the car park Michael glanced back at the Devil's Chair. Something up there moved. Black. A dog. A big black dog

bounded out from between two rocks and stood and stared at Michael.

Michael's heartbeat quickened.

A raven, a toad or a black dog.

"Michael!" Mr Ashton called.

Michael turned. When he looked back, the dog had vanished. Stupid, he told himself. Just a  dog. But where had it come from?

Back at the car park they saw that several more cars had appeared. Michael was reassured. The dog must have belonged to some visitors; it was a family pet.

They drove back to school, chattering, comparing drawings, sucking sweets. Michael boasted about his experiment, showing off his cuts and bruises.

"Didn't see the Devil, though, did we?" said Paul.

"There was a dog – a black dog," protested Michael, and immediately felt a chill, remembering the way the dog had appeared as if from nowhere.

"I never saw it," said Paul.

But Jane definitely had. She looked frightened.

When they arrived back at school it was only half past two. Mr Ashton said they could spend the last hour finishing their drawings or writing about the visit.

The children sighed; they were hot and restless and all they wanted was to go home.

Michael began drawing. He'd looked up at the Devil's Chair so often as he climbed around it that he thought he could draw it from memory. He quickly drew the shape of the granite throne and the tumbled rocks beneath.

When he looked at his finished picture he was pleased. It was good. But –

94

what was that? A dark shape half hidden behind one of the boulders? Something hiding. A dog? He hadn't drawn that. Surely he hadn't. He rubbed it out. But then he thought he saw it again, behind another rock: a muzzle, the tip of an ear. He rubbed vigorously and drew more rocks to hide it.

Kelly said, "Sir, there's a dog on the playing field."

Michael stiffened. But the others, glad of a diversion from their work, jumped up with a scraping of chairs and jostled at the windows, as Mr Ashton struggled to retain order.

"Sit down, Paul, Craig. Sit down,

Zoe. It's just a dog. We've all seen dogs before." He paused by Michael's table. "That's coming on well, Michael."

Michael looked at his picture. What had he drawn? Was that a shadow behind the rocks in the foreground, or . . . ? He scrubbed with the rubber, and made a hole in the paper.

The class settled down. Quiet returned. Coughs, rustling paper, whispers.

And then a scream from Jane. "The dog!"

Michael leapt to his feet. Chairs toppled, voices erupted. The dog –

a great black hound – had reared up against the window, staring in. Mr Ashton banged on the glass and made shooing movements. The dog dropped down, out of sight, then sprang up again; its claws scraped on the glass, scraping and scratching; saliva hung from its jaws.

Michael stood rigid with fear. Some of the children whimpered; others began banging and shooing.

"Sit down, everyone," said Mr Ashton. "I'll get the caretaker." He went out.

When he came back Zoe said, "It's gone, Sir."

"Probably a stray," said Mr Ashton. It was nearly half past three. "Pack up your things."

Michael looked at his drawing. There were no shadows now, no odd shapes, and yet . . . The picture made him uneasy. He screwed it up and hurled it at the bin. Mr Ashton was startled. "Spoilt it," muttered Michael.

All the way home he watched for dogs. There were plenty of them, of course: terriers, Alsatians, collies, a Great Dane stately on a lead. Once, out of the corner of his eye, he thought he saw a black dog behind a wall; then, again, padding alongside a privet hedge. He ran, banged open the gate of his garden and beat on the front door.

"I'm not deaf," his mother said.

He was home, safe. He dumped his bag, got a drink and some crisps, settled in front of the television.

He stayed in all evening. He ate his dinner, scribbled some homework, then went back to the television. His favourite programmes washed over him, lulling and reassuring. He'd been imagining things. There were often dogs on the school playing field. And the streets were full of black dogs; it was simply that he was noticing them more today. That one behind the privet hedge, for instance: surely that was Caesar, the Wilsons' labrador? Stupid. He'd been really stupid.

He felt sleepy. The cuts on his hands smarted.

"You all right?" His mother felt his forehead.

"Tired. It was hot on the trip. We walked miles."

"You'd better get an early night."

Michael thought with unusual longing of his bedroom with its posters and comics, his Mickey Mouse alarm clock and his Batman duvet cover.

"Okay," he said.

He went slowly upstairs.

"Wash," said his mother. "Don't forget."

Michael washed briefly, leaving grubby prints on the towel. His head ached. He was sleepy, so sleepy.

He stumbled across the landing and pushed open his bedroom door.

Huge, on the bed, lay the black dog. Waiting.

Bush Medicine

Faustin Charles

Milton Codrington was a bachelor. He lived in a one-roomed house in St Victoria village, Barbados. He was a poor, simple man, who didn't have a job nor a trade.

One night he had a dream that was to change his whole life. In his dream, Milton saw an old woman picking pawpaw leaves, putting them into a boiling pot, stirring the brew and saying, "Boil for a hour, wait till it cool, then drink, good for all kinda sickness."

The dream ended, Milton turned, opened his eyes, sat up in bed, then he muttered, "Pawpaw leaf. I never realize ordinary pawpaw leaf so good for medicine."

So Milton went to a pawpaw tree in the backyard of his house, picked

 some leaves, boiled them in a pan for an hour, then he said, "Now, how I going to know whether this brew work or not, I not

sick with nothing?"

Just then a neighbour, Ma Gerty, called to him. "Milton, boy, me granddaughter sick bad bad with the flu, and I don't know what to do!"

Milton poured some of the pawpaw-leaf brew into a cup and gave it to Ma Gerty, and said, "It's like bush tea, but don't put no sugar in it, just give it to you granddaughter to drink."

Ma Gerty stared at the dark-green liquid, nodded, and said, "Boy, I ain't have much faith in these bush medicine, but I going give this to she, and thank you." And she went and gave it to her granddaughter.

 About fifteen minutes later, Ma Gerty shouted from her house, "Milton, boy! It work! The girl better. Praise the Lord!" Ma Gerty was laughing and kissing her granddaughter who was sitting up in bed, smiling.

"Yes, praise the Lord!" Milton grinned. "I tell you it woulda make she better!"

Soon Milton was giving the pawpaw bush medicine to the whole village. Then people started coming to him from all over the island. Whenever anyone became ill, instead

of first going to the doctor or the
hospital, they went to Milton for his
pawpaw-leaf brew, and they were
cured of all their illnesses. Milton
was convinced that the pawpaw-leaf
brew was a magic cure and he told
no one about how he came by it. He
felt that he was specially chosen by
God to have the knowledge about
the pawpaw-leaf medicine.

Milton's fame as the man with the
magic cure spread
to other islands.

He was a vain man, and loved the respect he was getting from all quarters. He took no money for his brew. People gave him food and clothes, that was all he would accept.

Ma Gerty always stood on the veranda of her house watching all the goings-on.

One day, when most of the people had gone away from Milton's house, two men from the city of Bridgetown came to see him. One was called Riley, who owned a dry-goods shop, and the other, Franklyn, was a chemist.

"Now what can I do for all you?" Milton asked.

"Well, it's like this, Mr Codrington," answered Riley. "We hear about you bush medicine, and we was wondering if you interested in going into business."

"Business like what?" Milton asked.

"What we mean is this," Franklyn said calmly. "You bush medicine is popular all over the islands. Now suppose you make it and we bottle it and market it and sell it. We can make a lotta money, the three of we together."

Milton looked bewildered.

"You can have big, big house, car and servants and plenty other nice things," said Franklyn.

"Money mean power, you know," said Riley.

Milton smiled a little. "I always thought that bush medicine is free for all," he said. "After all, bush growing wild all over the place. People pick it and try it, if it work then they use it and tell others about it. They does never charge money for it."

"I know I was wasting me time coming here, yes," Riley raged. "The man making sport, man. It's people like you who does end up begging by the roadside, and when people check back at you life, they discover that you had a chance of becoming rich and you didn't take it."

"Riley, man, I tell you don't get on so," Franklyn pleaded.

"How you want me to get on!" Riley snapped. "The man must be crazy, that's all."

"That's not the way to talk to people, man," said Franklyn who was becoming fed up with the whole idea. "You must control youself."

"All right, all right, man, I sorry," Riley said coolly.

Milton wiped his face with a dingy piece of red cloth, and studied the two men carefully. Then he said, "All right, I go do it with all you."

Riley laughed and said, "Now you talking sense, man."

"You see when you give people time to make up they mind, everything does work out all right," Franklyn smiled.

"Now, you must stop giving away the brew free to people, you hear," said Riley. "When they come and ask you for it you must tell them, 'All freeness done.'"

"All right, then," Milton nodded.

"It going to be hard, but I go stop giving it away."

"Mr Codrington, that'll be in the contract," said Franklyn, still smiling.

Milton felt a very strange feeling welling up in his stomach.

Milton went into business with Riley and Franklyn, and the business prospered. He now lived in a beautiful house with an extra large kitchen where he boiled the pawpaw-

leaf brew in large pots on an electric stove. He installed a telephone, and when the brew was ready he called

112

Riley or Franklyn and they sent a van to collect it.

They checked it, bottled and labelled it, and sold it. The profits from the business were split equally three ways.

Milton stopped giving the brew away to people who called at his home begging for it. He lied and said that he no longer made the brew, or that he had forgotten how to make it.

One morning, Ma Gerty called at his home. Milton looked out of a window and greeted her sheepishly. "Good morning, Ma. How life treating you these days?"

Ma Gerty was fuming. "Milton, what is this I hearing, that you not giving away the bush water to nobody no more. What happening?"

Milton tried to smile, but failed. "Ma, I stop making that. I ain't have no time with it. I doing big business with other things now."

"The other day, a woman come to you for some of the bush water and you tell she, no, you don't make it no more," Ma Gerty said. "That woman did want the medicine for she sick baby, she didn't get it, and now she child dead. You know about that?"

Milton felt sick, and he began to shake all over. "Well, I sorry about that," he said timidly, "but as I say, I ain't making the bush brew no more, it's too much headache and worry, man."

"And what about them two fellas I see that come to see you some time ago?" Ma Gerty went on. "I know that one of them is a druggist, and the other one own a shop."

"Them is just me long-time friend, man," Milton gasped as his head ached. "I use to know them from me schooldays, and they did drop in to say howdy, that's all."

"Milton, I feel you up to something. I hope you know what you doing. You suddenly get rich overnight, you think people don't suspect you up to something, and something that not nice? You should have a little conscience, man; that woman child spirit going to haunt you."

"I don't know what you talking about, Ma, I does live a good life."

"Boy, you does get me so damn vex sometimes. All right, when bad luck start blighting you, don't come for my help, you hear!" Ma Gerty glared at him and went off.

And almost at once the bad luck did begin to blight.

As the days passed, Milton started
to change. His fingers and arms
began to look like the leaves and
stems of a pawpaw tree. His hair
grew long and dishevelled, and his
body resembled the trunk of the
tree. On the soles of his feet
grew tiny roots. His
whole body throbbed
with a burning pain,
and the colour of
his skin changed
from dark brown
to green. He was
ashamed and
afraid to go
outside his house

in the daytime. He drank large
quantities of the pawpaw-leaf brew,
hoping to get better and change
back to his normal self, but the more
he drank, the worse he became.

One night, when Milton was out
picking the pawpaw leaves, he felt a
great pain in his stomach; he
couldn't move from where he was
standing, and suddenly he was a
pawpaw tree.

The spirit of the dead child
entered the tree and it swayed in a
gentle breeze ...

A Loathly Lady

Susan Price

A long, long time ago and a while
before that, there were three brothers.
And the eldest of these three brothers,
he upped and said to his father, "I'm
off to seek my fortune." And away he
went, riding on a good horse, with a
good greyhound running behind, and
a good hawk on his arm. And neither
he, nor his horse, nor his greyhound,
nor his hawk were ever seen again.

Now the second brother saddled his horse, took his hawk on his arm, whistled up his greyhound, and rode off to search for the first brother, and maybe to find a fortune of his own. But he never came back either.

Now there was only the youngest brother left and, when he heard nothing from his two brothers, he upped and saddled his horse, took his hawk on his arm, called his greyhound, and rode off to search for them.

He rode by hill, he rode by dale, and

everyone he passed he asked for
news of his brothers. Yes, they said,
two young men had ridden this way
before him – and so he kicked his
horse and rode all the faster. Soon he
was lost in a forest and didn't know
how to go forward or back. But then
he saw a hall through the trees and
thought himself lucky. "Somewhere
to shelter for the night," he said to
his horse and his hound.

The hall was built of logs and
roofed with shingles, but the shutters
were hanging off, and the worm had
got into the wood. No one had lived
there for many years, and no one was
about now. The youngest brother

tethered his horse outside the hall, rubbed her down, threw his cloak over her, and left her to graze. Inside the hall, his hawk flew into the rafters to perch, and he built himself a fire and settled down beside it with his hound.

As the hours passed, the dark grew close about the little fire, and the cold draughts grew sharper. The loose shutters banged in the wind, and the trees outside could be heard lashing themselves with their branches. The wind blew in around the broken door, making the fire flicker and scattering the old, dried rushes about the floor. And then

 came a sound like
heavy tramping –
a thumping of big,
heavy feet –
coming out of the
forest: tramp,
thump, closer and
closer to the hall where the man and
dog lay huddled together.

Thump! Tramp! Suddenly the
doorway was filled by a dark shape.
It ducked its head and into the
firelight came a giantess, a hag, a
monster – the ugliest old harridan
you ever saw.

How can I tell you about her? Her
hair was grey and hung down in

greasy strings, so greasy it seemed her hair was soaking wet; and her skin was as greasy and grey as her hair. Red with blood her eyes were, with crusts of yellow matter at the corners, and the lower lids sagged to show wet red linings. And so crossed were her eyes that she could only see the swollen end of her puffy red nose – from which ropes of thick yellow snot hung to her chest. Her lips wouldn't close over her three yellow teeth, and she drooled.

Her spine was curved as much as a bent bow, and her big-knuckled, broken-nailed hands hung down by her bandy knees. The horny yellow nails on her toes were hard and sharp as flint and cut pieces out of the floor as she crossed it. And the smell of her! The smell that rolled off her as she came! The smell would choke a fox; it would curdle a cesspit; it would make a stone crumble.

This loathly lady came to the fireside, and she looked at the youngest brother and she said, "Food, give me food."

The reek of her as she came close made even the fire shrink back. Strings of snot and drool hung from her face and tangled in her greasy hair. But her eyes, though they were red and sore, were so sad as she looked at him, as if she knew too well her own ugliness. The young man was afraid, but he could not bring himself to say anything that would make her eyes sadder. "If I had food, lady," he said, "I would share it with you gladly. But I have no food with me – I had hoped to be out of this forest before night."

The greyhound at his side was curling its lips at the hag, and growling. She looked down at it. "Food," she said.

"My good dog, lady."

"Meat," she said.

And her eyes were so sad, and her ugliness so gaunt, that it hurt the young man to refuse her the only food there was in the hall – yet it hurt him, too, to think of his good dog, which had loved and trusted him so long, being gobbled by that drooling mouth.

"Food," said the loathly lady, and whimpered. "Food," she said, and tears ran from her sore, sad, blood-red eyes.

"Take him, then," said the young man, and scrambled up from his place

beside the fire and turned his back.
Behind him he heard his dog snarl,
and then shriek; and then a sound of
breaking and gobbling, of tearing
and gulping. And the young man put
his hands to his face to catch the hot
tears that spilled for his poor dog –
and he could not tell if he did right
to feed one poor hungry creature by
ending the life of another.

Then the loathly lady spoke again.
"More meat," she said.

The young man turned to find her
looking up into the rafters at his
hawk which perched there. "My
pretty hawk – she will only be a
mouthful to you."

"More meat," said the loathly lady, and stared at him through hair and snot and grime with sad, sad red eyes.

With tears running down his own face, the young man raised his wrist and whistled, and the hawk flew down to him, fanning his face with air from her wings. She had hardly alighted before the lady snatched her away and crammed her whole into her mouth. The young man closed his eyes and turned away, and in a moment the hawk was eaten: bones and feathers and guts and all.

"More meat, more meat," said the loathly lady.

"There is only my poor horse."

"More meat," she said. So the young man went out into the night, untethered his horse, and led her back into the hall. He turned his face to the wall while the lady ate her, skin and bones and hair and guts and all.

And if she asks for more meat, and there is only myself, he thought, *how can I refuse her when I gave her my dog, my hawk and my horse?*

But the next thing the lady said was, "A bed. A bed." Her tears splashed holes in the dirt floor. "Let me lie down and rest these long tired bones. Make me a bed."

The young man went out again and used his sword to cut soft green ferns. He carried them back in armfuls and made with them a deep bed, over which he spread his cloak now that his horse needed it no longer. "Your bed, lady."

She lay down on the bed, and sighed, so glad was she to rest at last. "Now come and kiss me," she said.

To kiss that face besmeared with snot and drool, to have his own face besmeared by the grease of that rank hair – it made the young man tremble.

But the sad, sad eyes stared at him,
and he felt great pity for her. So he
kissed her cheek – and fell
senseless, stunned
by her stink.

He woke
when the
sun shone in
through the broken
shutter and around the ill-
fitting door. When he turned his
head, he saw sleeping beside him the
most beautiful girl that his eyes, or
mine, or yours, had ever seen. Her
hair spread over her shoulders, red-
gold, shining. Her face was smooth
and lovely, and her eyes a clear blue.

She smiled, and she had all her teeth, and they were small and white.

She kissed him and said, "You gave me your dog, you gave me your hawk, you gave me your horse. And still more, you made me a bed and covered it with your cloak. But more still, you gave me a kiss, all to please me, ugly and frightening as I was. And now I give you myself, and my land, for I know your heart is gentle and your eyes see more than is before them. You will make a fine king."

And he looked about and saw a hall that was no longer a ruin, and was filled with rich things and comforts. And it would be easy to say that he made a fine king, and lived happily ever after with his beautiful queen.

But when he saw her smile, he remembered the hag's teeth crunching on the bones of his good dog, his hawk, his horse. And whatever became of his two brothers, who had ridden into the forest before him?

The beauty was a hag, and the hag was a beauty, and knowing that doesn't let you sleep peacefully at night.

Mine

Anthony Masters

On the wind, Jo heard someone call her name. She got off her mountain bike and listened. For a while she could hear only a curlew call. The bracken rustled, the ugly sheets of tin fencing round the old mine shaft rattled and a light plane buzzed like a mosquito in the Indian-summer sky. White clouds raced above her and the moor smelt sweet.

"Jo."

She started. The
call was quite clear
now and there was
an urgency to it.
"Jo."

She laid her bike down on the
worn track and walked across to the
old mine shaft that had been securely
closed off years ago – though a
couple of the fencing sheets had
been wrenched away by the fierce
winds that had been raging over the
moorland for the last few days. A
warning notice lay flat on the rough
tussocky grass a few feet away from
the shaft.

DANGER. DO NOT ENTER.
DISUSED MINE WORKING.

Then the voice came again.

"Who's there?" Jo asked nervously.

There was no reply – only the distant bleating of a sheep and the wailing of the gusty wind amongst the tin sheeting.

"Jo." Faintly she heard the call again.

"Who is it?"

"Come on, Jo!" This time the words were very distinct.

Jo hesitated. Hadn't she been warned about this old mine? Wasn't everyone

meant to keep clear of it? Suppose
someone was in trouble, though,
someone she could help. Besides,
wasn't there something familiar
about that voice?

She walked through the gap.

Below her the shaft yawned – dim,
desolate and overgrown with
brambles. Wooden boarding that had
originally covered the abyss hung in
rotten shards. Looking down, Jo
could see only darkness. Then, as her
eyes became accustomed to the dark,
she could make out grey rock and a
ledge that sloped gently upwards.

This was the place where they
had brought them out, her memory

told her. Uncle Jack, cousin Jem, and her father's mate Billy.

All killed in the pit disaster before Jo had been born. She had often cycled up here, curious about the dead men. Of course, she'd seen photographs, but what had they really been like?

"Jo. What are you doing, lass? What's keeping you?"

Jo stared down into the void and the familiar memory stirred in her mind. "They never found

your Grandad, Jo, however much they dug." That's why she came up here really, to be with the grandfather she had never known.

"Come on, Jo. What's keeping you?"

"But who are you?"

"Some of my mates are trapped. Can you get down?" The voice was urgent now. "I've been trying to find a way out – a way out for us all. You've got to help me." The urgency increased.

"The way out's up here," said Jo desperately.

"I can't see anything – none of us can."

"I'll get help."

"No time. You coming, Jo?"

An instinct drove her on as she slithered down to the ledge, knowing what she was doing was crazy, but unable to stop herself.

Still she couldn't see anything – just a black pit with what looked like sheer sides. She called down into it.

"Hello?"

There was no reply.

"Oi!"

Still no reply.

"Where are you?"

The silence was like a wall. Then Jo felt the rock crumbling beneath her feet, breaking up. She pitched into the darkness.

Her shoulder hit something hard and the painful vibration echoed right through her body. Jo lay there shaking, not daring to move in case she plummeted further down, closing her eyes against the horror of it all, curling herself up into a womb-like shape, cursing her own stupidity. Obviously she had imagined the voice. She must have done. Then, in her mounting fear, she hoped she hadn't, hoped against hope that there was someone there to help her.

"Where are you?"
she whispered,
then shouted.

Still no reply.
Jo shifted,
reached out a hand, and froze as
grim reality swept over her. She was
on another ledge – this time
narrower – and the void again
stretched below to a seemingly
endless depth. Her shoulder hurt and
she groaned with pain. Then, deep in
the shaft below, Jo heard answering
groans. So she wasn't on her own!
Involuntarily, she moved backwards –
and encountered solid, warm, human
flesh. Jo screamed again and again.

"What's happening? What's happening?"

"You've got to help me, lass."

They were lying side by side – Jo and whoever it was. She could smell sweat mingled with coal-dust.

"I got up here – trying to find a way out. The others are down below. Dying, most of them. But some might live – if we can help them." He gasped slightly.

"Are you hurt?"

"Can't breathe – not that well. But I'll be all right."

The groaning below continued, and then someone began to pray in a high, keening voice.

"There's a way out," said Jo. "Up there."

"I can't see anything. Must be dust in the eyes."

Jo turned to him at last, summoning up all her courage, but all she could see was a dark shape, half-buried under an overhanging lip of rock.

"I can see the light," she said. "I think we could climb to there." She stared up at the pale sky, which seemed a very long way above her.

"You'll have to help me."

"Okay." Trembling, Jo clambered to her feet, her shoulder pounding with pain.

"Can you stand?" she asked her

companion.

"I don't know."

"Try."

Jo searched for and found a gnarled hand. She pulled and felt an answering weight. It dragged at her at first and then seemed not to be there.

"Where are you?"

"Here, lass." A gaunt shape was standing silently beside her and suddenly Jo felt the deathly chill of the wrist she was holding. She dropped it with a cry, the chill becoming ice, burning into her flesh. "Can't see nothing." The voice was distant now, almost like a sigh in the darkness, and Jo began to shake, the coldness spreading inside her so that she could hardly bear the pain.

"Can't see a thing."

"The light's up there."

"I'll take your word for it. Show me where to climb."

"It's steep. I don't know if we'll manage it."

The drifting voice became sharper. "Look lively, lass, there's dying men down there."

"Give me your hand again."

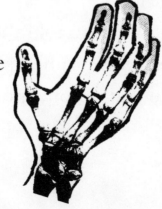

For a moment she felt cobweb fingers. Then they passed through her own.

"Anyone down there?" The voice broke into the emptiness with unexpected harshness.

There was a face above her; a man with a helmet.

"Who are you?" Jo croaked, as if she hadn't spoken for a very long time. She was still shuddering all over and there was cold sweat on her forehead.

"Police. We were told the workings were open so we came up. Then I saw a bike and no one around. Are you hurt?"

"My shoulder, but it's not too bad. There are other people down here."

"Other people? How many?"

"I don't know. There's been a cave-in."

"What?"

"They're saying prayers. And there's a man beside me."

"Is there?" Her rescuer's voice was reassuring and sympathetic as the powerful beam of his torch swept the ledge. "I can't see anyone."

Jo turned quickly back to her companion. There was no one there, but she could make out something lying in the shadows. She leaned down and picked it up while the torch beam again doused the rock in brilliant white light. It was a miner's helmet, dented a little on its dome just above the flashlight, the way it was in the photograph she had seen. She stared at it.

"Hang on," said the policeman. "My mate's coming with a rope – and I'm going

to lower him down to you. We'll
have you up in no time."

"What about the others?"

"We'll get to them," the policeman
replied in the same quiet, calm voice.

"Where are you?" called Jo.

There was no reply.

"Who are you?"

Still no reply.

A few seconds later, another
policeman came down to her on
a rope.

"I'm just going to slip this harness
round your waist," he began.

"Wait."

"No time for that, lass." There was
an edge to his voice and a certain

unsteadiness. "There could be
another rock fall any moment."

"What's that under the rock?"

He swept the dark cavity with his
torch. "Could be a skeleton," he said
uncertainly. "Yes . . . yes, I think it is.

We'll look into that later." The policeman gulped, clearly wanting to get out of there as quickly as possible. "Come on!"

As Jo was swung up in the harness, she cradled the miner's helmet in her arms.

"This was my grandad's," she said to herself. "And now it's mine."

Acknowledgements

"A Face in the Dark" copyright © **Ruskin Bond** 1994;
"Bush Medicine" copyright © **Faustin Charles** 1994;
"Tsipporah" copyright © **Adèle Geras** 1994;
"The Bravest Man in the World" copyright © **Robert Hull** 1994; "Mine" copyright © **Anthony Masters** 1994; "The Oddment" copyright © **Chris Powling** 1994; "A Loathly Lady" copyright © **Susan Price** 1994;
"Things That Go Bump in the Day" copyright © **Tony Ross** 1989; "Widdershins" copyright © **Ann Turnbull** 1994.